Illustrated by Beccy Blake

W
FRANKLIN WATTS
LONDON • SYDNEY

Notes on the series

TIDDLERS are structured to provide support for children who are starting to read on their own. The stories may also be used for sharing with children.

Starting to read alone can be daunting. **TIDDLERS** help by listing the words in the book for a check before reading, and by providing visual support and repeating words and phrases. These books will both develop confidence and encourage reading and rereading for pleasure.

If you are reading this book with a child, here are a few suggestions:

1. Make reading fun! Choose a time to read when you and the child are relaxed and have time to share the story.
2. Talk about the story before you start reading. Look at the cover and the blurb. What might the story be about? Why might the child like it?
3. Look also at the list of words below – can the child tackle most of the words? Encourage the child to employ a phonics approach to tackling new words by sounding the words out.
4. Encourage the child to retell the story, using the jumbled picture puzzle.
5. Give praise! Remember that small mistakes need not always be corrected.

Here is a list of the words in this story.

Common words:

all	in	stop
at	is	the
can	off	then
he	red	they
I	said	

Other words:

Alf	hear	Sid
car	looked	squeaks
engine	seems	under
fine	set	wife

"Stop, Sid!"

SID

4

Sid looked in the car.

Alf looked under
the car.

"All seems fine,"
Sid said.

Then he set off.

"Stop, Sid!
I can hear
squeaks."

11

Sid looked at
the engine.

"All seems fine,"
Sid said.

Then he set off.

"Stop!" said Sid's wife.

17

"I can hear squeaks."

"All is fine!"
they said.

Puzzle Time

Can you find these pictures in the story?

Which pages are the
pictures from?

Turn over for answers!

Answers

The pictures come
from these pages:

a. pages 10–11

b. pages 4–5

c. pages 12–13

d. pages 18–19

Franklin Watts
First published in Great Britain in 2016 by
The Watts Publishing Group

Copyright (text) © Hilary Robinson 2016
Copyright (illustration) © Beccy Blake 2016

The rights of Hilary Robinson to be
identified as the author and Beccy Blake to
be identified as the illustrator of this Work
have been asserted in accordance with the
Copyright, Designs and Patents Act, 1988.

Series Editor: Jackie Hamley
Series Advisor: Catherine Glavina
Series Designer: Cathryn Gilbert

A CIP catalogue record for this book is
available from the British Library.

ISBN 978 1 4451 4597 6 (hbk)
ISBN 978 1 4451 4599 0 (pbk)
ISBN 978 1 4451 4598 3 (library ebook)

Printed in China

Franklin Watts
An imprint of
Hachette Children's Group
Part of The Watts Publishing Group
Carmelite House
50 Victoria Embankment
London EC4Y 0DZ

An Hachette UK Company
www.hachette.co.uk

www.franklinwatts.co.uk

FSC
www.fsc.org
MIX
Paper from
responsible sources
FSC® C104740